MOON CAMP

BARRY GOTT

VIKING

I had my summer vacation all planned out: sleeping in, playing video games, and having a whole lot of fun.

But THEN . . .

Mom and Dad signed me up for Moon Camp.

I do NOT want to go to the moon. There's no video games or oxygen or ANYTHING fun.

Moon Camp is going to be terrible, I just know it.

The launch makes my guts feel
like squished oatmeal.
I can hear my teeth chattering
over the roar of the engines.

When we land, I'm the last one off the rocket.
I don't know where I'm supposed to go.

I trip on a crater and spill my stuff everywhere.

By the time I catch up with the others, the sign-up lists for ALL my favorite activities are completely full.

SPACE RACING
Mally   Finn
Jason   Ethan
PAUL   Makayla
Julia   Isaac

MOON-BALL
Eli   Danny
Claire   Tyler
Sav   Lily
Zach   Anna

LASER ARCHERY
Gaby   Nandi
Aly   Tyler
Matt   Josh
Nate   Evan
Aaliyah Wyatt

LOOKING AT ROCKS
___   ___
___   ___
___   ___
___   ___
___   ___

My canoe springs a leak.

I think I'm allergic to moon dust.

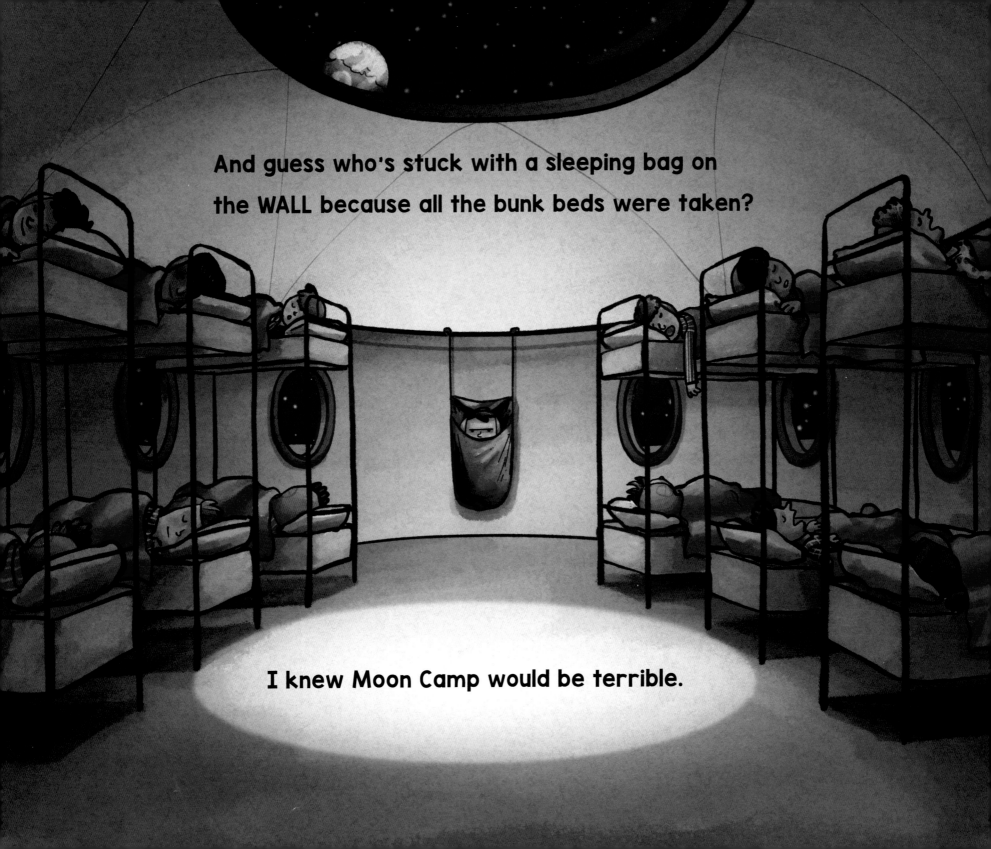

The eggs and bacon at breakfast are
NOT the way my mom makes them.

I even got lost during the group nature hike!

But you know what the worst
part of Moon Camp is?

I miss my mom and my dad and my planet.

Another rocket lands with more campers.
The kids all run off toward camp—all but
the last one, that is.

It seems like he's having . . .

. . . a terrible day.

AH-CHOO!!!

We grab his stuff and run to sign up for some fun activities. And hey—

Then we're off to get some moon dust allergy medicine at the nurse's office—where we make an amazing discovery!

Next we go to lunch. Sam has a great idea for how to make astronaut food taste better!

We pick out one of the good canoes together, and make it even more awesome!

And it turns out that sleeping on the wall is way more fun in a super-double-decker blanket fort!

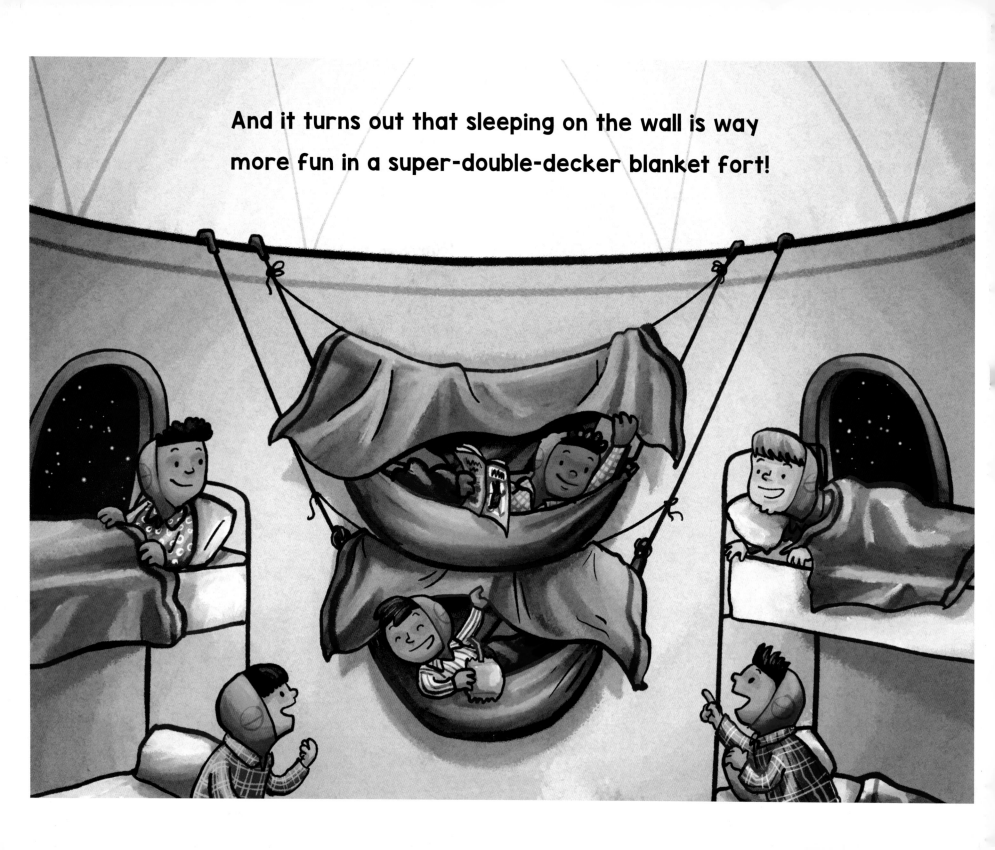

Even nature hikes are looking up!

On top of the biggest rock, Sam yells:

THE MOON IS AMAZING!

And you know what?

He's right!

On the last night of camp, we have a humongous bonfire, roast hot dogs (with lots of chocolate syrup!), and sing songs late into the night.

On the trip back to Earth, it turns out
we ALL forgot our gravity belts. Oops.

But I also forget to feel barfy!

When we land, Sam and I are the first ones off the rocket.

I'm so glad to be back with my mom and my dad and my planet . . .

But I also miss my friends and my moon—I can't wait till next summer!

For Rose, Finn, and Nandi

VIKING

An imprint of Penguin Random House LLC, New York

First published in the United States of America by Viking,
an imprint of Penguin Random House LLC, 2021

Visit us online at penguinrandomhouse.com.

Library of Congress Cataloging-in-Publication Data is available.

Manufactured in China

ISBN 9780593202678

1 3 5 7 9 10 8 6 4 2

Design by Lucia Baez and Barry Gott • Text set in Blank Space
The art was created in Clip Studio Paint.